D0103577

YSTERI

What Kids Say About Carole Marsh Mysteries . . .

I love the real locations! Reading the book always makes me want to go and visit them all on our next family vacation. My Mom says maybe, but I can't wait!

One day, I want to be a real kid in one of Ms. Marsh's mystery books. I think it would be fun, and I think I am a real character anyway. I filled out the application and sent it in and am keeping my fingers crossed!

History was not my favorite subject till I starting reading Carole Marsh Mysteries. Ms. Marsh really brings history to life. Also, she leaves room for the scary and fun.

I think Christina is so smart and brave. She is lucky to be in the mystery books because she gets to go to a lot of places. I always wonder just how much of the book is true and what is made up. Trying to figure that out is fun!

Grant is cool and funny! He makes me laugh a lot!!

I like that there are boys and girls in the story of different ages. Some mysteries I outgrow, but I can always find a favorite character to identify with in these books.

They are scary, but not too scary. They are funny. I learn a lot. There is always food which makes me hungry. I feel like I am there.

WEST BRANCH
PEABODY

JUN   2011

What Parents and Teachers Say About Carole Marsh Mysteries . . .

I think kids love these books because they have such a wealth of detail. I know I learn a lot reading them! It's an engaging way to look at the history of any place or event. I always say I'm only going to read one chapter to the kids, but that never happens—it's always two or three, at least!
—Librarian

Reading the mystery and going on the field trip—Scavenger Hunt in hand—was the most fun our class ever had! It really brought the place and its history to life. They loved the real kids characters and all the humor. I loved seeing them learn that reading is an experience to enjoy!
—4th grade teacher

Carole Marsh is really on to something with these unique mysteries. They are so clever; kids want to read them all. The Teacher's Guides are chock full of activities, recipes, and additional fascinating information. My kids thought I was an expert on the subject—and with this tool, I felt like it!
—3rd grade teacher

My students loved writing their own Real Kids/Real Places mystery book! Ms. Marsh's reproducible guidelines are a real jewel. They learned about copyright and more & ended up with their own book they were so proud of!
—Reading/Writing Teacher

"The kids seem very realistic—my children seemed to relate to the characters. Also, it is educational by expanding their knowledge about the famous places in the books."

"They are what children like: mysteries and adventures with children they can relate to."

"Encourages reading for pleasure."

"This series is great. It can be used for reluctant readers, and as a history supplement."

The Mystery on the

Great Wall of China

Beijing, China

by Carole Marsh

Copyright ©2006 Carole Marsh/ Gallopade International

Fourth Printing January 2010

All rights reserved.

Carole Marsh Mysteries™ and its skull colophon are the property of Carole Marsh and Gallopade International.

Published by Gallopade International/Carole Marsh Books. Printed in the United States of America.

The publisher would like to thank the following for their kind permission to reproduce the cover photographs.

Lauren Baker, New York, NY *Ancient Chinese Tablet;*
© **Seet Clarence, Singapore | Dreamstime.com** *Lantern Festival Dragon;*
© **Diane Diederich** *Fortune Cookie;*
© **2006 JupiterImages Corporation** *Fireworks, The Forbidden City, The Great Wall of China*

Managing Editor: Sherry Moss

Cover Design: Michele Winkelman

Content Design: Steven St. Laurent, Line Creek Creative

Gallopade International is introducing SAT words that kids need to know in each new book that we publish. The SAT words are bold in the story. Look for this special logo beside each word in the glossary. Happy Learning!

Gallopade is proud to be a member and supporter of these educational organizations and associations:

American Booksellers Association
American Library Association
International Reading Association
National Association for Gifted Children
The National School Supply and Equipment Association
The National Council for the Social Studies
Museum Store Association
Association of Partners for Public Lands
Association of Booksellers for Children
Association for the Study of African American Life and History
National Alliance of Black School Educators

This book is a complete work of fiction. All events are fictionalized, and although the names of real people are used, their characterization in this book is fiction. All attractions, product names, or other works mentioned in this book are trademarks of their respective owners and the names and images used in this book are strictly for editorial purposes; no commercial claims to their use is claimed by the author or publisher.

Without limiting the rights under copyright reserved above, no part of this publication may be reproduced, stored in or introduced into a retrieval system, or transmitted, in any form or by any means (electronic, mechanical, photocopying, recording or otherwise), without the prior written permission of both the copyright owner and the above publisher of this book.

The scanning, uploading, and distribution of this book via the Internet or via any other means without the permission of the publisher is illegal and punishable by law. Please purchase only authorized electronic editions and do not participate in or encourage electronic piracy of copyrightable materials. Your support of the author's rights is appreciated.

30 Years Ago . . .

As a mother and an author, one of the fondest periods of my life was when I decided to write mystery books for children. At this time (1979) kids were pretty much glued to the TV, something parents and teachers complained about the way they do about web surfing and blogging today.

I decided to set each mystery in a real place—a place kids could go and visit for themselves after reading the book. And I also used real children as characters. Usually a couple of my own children served as characters, and I had no trouble recruiting kids from the book's location to also be characters.

Also, I wanted all the kids—boys and girls of all ages—to participate in solving the mystery. And, I wanted kids to learn something as they read. Something about the history of the location. And I wanted the stories to be funny. That formula of real+scary+smart+fun served me well.

I love getting letters from teachers and parents who say they read the book with their class or child, then visited the historic site and saw all the places in the mystery for themselves. What's so great about that? What's great is that you and your children have an experience that bonds you together forever. Something you shared. Something you both cared about at the time. Something that crossed all age levels—a good story, a good scare, a good laugh!

30 years later,

Carole Marsh

Christina "Mystery Girl"   Mimi   Papa   Grant

Hey, kids! As you see—here we are ready to embark on another of our exciting Carole Marsh Mystery adventures! You know, in "real life," I keep very close tabs on Christina, Grant, and their friends when we travel. However, in the mystery books, they always seem to slip away from me and Papa so that they can try to solve the mystery on their own!

I hope you will go to www.carolemarshmysteries.com and apply to be a character in a future mystery book! Well, the *Mystery Girl* is all tuned up and ready for "take-off!"

Gotta go... Papa says so! Wonder what I've forgotten this time?

Happy "Armchair Travel" Reading,

Mimi

About the Characters

Christina, age 10: Mysterious things really do happen to her! Hobbies: soccer, Girl Scouts, anything crafty, hanging out with Mimi, and going on new adventures.

Grant, age 7: Always manages to fall off boats, back into cactuses, and find strange clues—even in real life! Hobbies: camping, baseball, computer games, math, and hanging out with Papa.

Mimi is Carole Marsh, children's book author and creator of Carole Marsh Mysteries, Around the World in 80 Mysteries, Three Amigos Mysteries, Criss, Cross, Applesauce Detective Agency Mysteries, and many others.

Papa is Bob Longmeyer, the author's real-life husband, who really does wear a tuxedo, cowboy boots and hat, fly an airplane, captain a boat, speak in a booming voice, and laugh a lot!

Travel around the world with Christina and Grant as they visit famous places in 80 countries, and experience the mysterious happenings that always seem to follow them!

Books in This Series

#1 The Mystery at Big Ben
(London, England)

#2 The Mystery at the Eiffel Tower
(Paris, France)

#3 The Mystery at the Roman Colosseum
(Rome, Italy)

#4 The Mystery of the Ancient Pyramid
(Cairo, Egypt)

#5 The Mystery on the Great Wall of China
(Beijing, China)

#6 The Mystery on the Great Barrier Reef
(Australia)

#7 The Mystery at Mt. Fuji
(Tokyo, Japan)

#8 The Mystery in the Amazon Rainforest
(South America)

#9 The Mystery at Dracula's Castle
(Transylvania, Romania)

#10 The Curse of the Acropolis
(Athens, Greece)

#11 The Mystery at the Crystal Castle
(Bavaria, Germany)

#12 The Mystery in Icy Antarctica

#13 The Rip-Roaring Mystery on the African Safari
(South Africa)

#14 The Breathtaking Mystery on Mount Everest
(The Top of the World)

Table of Contents

1 A Slow Boat to China 1
2 Confucious Say... 7
3 Pen Pals. 11
4 One Hump, or Two?. 17
5 A Treasure Map! 21
6 A Ride in a Rickshaw. 27
7 Face-to-Face with a Dragon! 31
8 The Forbidden City. 33
9 The Hong Kong Express. 41
10 The "Flowerpot" Army 47
11 Hung Up in Hong Kong. 51
12 Somewhere Over China 55
13 Let the Fireworks Begin! 63
14 Victoria Peak. 69
15 Vanished!. 75
16 Star Ferry 79
17 Leaving Kowloon. 85
18 Good Luck Charms. 89
19 Beware!. 93
20 Missing!. 99
21 The Great Wall 103
22 X Marks the Spot!. 109
23 A Race to the Treasure! 115
24 The Jade Thief. 119
25 How You Gonna Keep 'Em Down on the Farm, After
    They've Seen the Great Wall?. 123

About the Author 127
Built-In Book Club: Talk About It! 128
Built-In Book Club: Bring it to Life! 130
Glossary 132

A Slow Boat to China

"Mimi," Christina asked, "are you going to write a mystery set in China?"

Christina's grandmother just continued to stare out the Air China airplane window with a dreamy look in her eyes.

"Mimi?" Christina repeated. "Mimi?"

"Oh, I heard you," Mimi finally answered. "How can I?" she asked her granddaughter. "China is so...so...well, just look!"

The four heads of Mimi, Papa, Christina, and Grant huddled together to stare out at the enormous mountain range far beneath them. Traversing the hillsides was a long—indeed, endless, or at least as far as they could see in either direction—stone snake.

"The Great Wall of China," Papa intoned in his deep, cowboy voice.

"*Great* seems like a small word for it," Mimi agreed breathlessly.

Christina shook her head sadly. "We'll never get to see all of China, will we?"

"Not in all our lifetimes put together," admitted Mimi.

Grant pressed his nose against the glass. "Well, can we at least walk the Great Wall?" he asked hopefully.

Papa laughed. "Just part of it, or all the *thousands* of miles of it?"

Christina and Grant gasped together. They knew that China was one of the largest and most mysterious and exotic countries in the world. They'd heard Mimi talk about its history of emperors and dynasties and culture. Papa said that with its billions of people, it was an important trade partner with the United States and other countries.

"Mimi," Christina said, "I think you're right—you probably can't write a mystery big enough to get all of China in it."

"What?" squealed Grant. "But I already told our pen pals Li and Cong that you would. In fact," he added, blushing, "I, uh, I told them that they could be characters in the book."

"Grant!" scolded Christina. "You know Mimi only picks kids who go to her fan club website and apply to be a character."

"But they did!" Grant argued. "A long time ago, back when we first started writing postcards to each other."

"Oh, that's right," said Christina. "I remember now. Li said she would be a good character because she was cute and sweet and smart in school and loves to read mysteries in Chinese *and* English."

"And Cong said he was good at figuring out clues, and he knows martial arts, and he likes to break rules," Grant added.

"Just what we need," grumbled Papa, "more little rule breakers." He pointed to Christina and Grant and grinned. "And why do you two varmints think you make such good mystery book characters?"

Now Grant and Christina grinned. "Because we're your grandkids, of course!"

Christina tugged at Mimi's sleeve. "So will you write a mystery about China, please?"

Mimi just continued to stare out the window at the magnificent landscape below. "Sure," she finally agreed in a dreamy voice. "Just get me off this airplane and put me on a slow boat to China...and I'll be done in a few hundred years."

When the red lights flashed FASTEN SEATBELTS in preparation for landing, Grant and Christina hopped back across the aisle into their own seats.

"Christina," Grant whispered. "We can't wait that long for a new book—we'll be old and gray. We've got to help Mimi."

"How?" Christina asked, shaking her head.

Grant stared out the window. "By helping her find a mystery—real quick. REAL QUICK!"

"Grant," Christina said, "I don't think you find a mystery, I think *it* finds *you*."

Grant looked back out the window as China rushed up at them as they began their descent. *Oh, no,* he thought to himself. *I will find Mimi a mystery. I can find Mimi a mystery. China is so mysterious that I'll bet I find a mystery even before we even get off...*

Suddenly, Grant spied something peculiar in the seatback pocket. While his sister filled out her immigration papers and admired her passport picture one more time, he gently pulled a ragged piece of old parchment paper out of the pocket. When he looked closely at it, he grinned. It was a treasure map, complete with plenty of directions, an X to mark the spot where the treasure could be found, and even a skull and crossbones warning. Or was that a dragon?

Quickly, Grant folded the map and tucked it his pocket. He smiled a little secret smile. *Wait until Christina, Li, and Cong see this! Of course, it is all in Chinese, but that will make the mystery even more fun to solve—won't it?*

Confucius Say...

Papa had been pretty disappointed that he hadn't been able to fly the *Mystery Girl,* his little red and white airplane, into China. That's how they usually traveled around, or either on Papa's green and white boat, also named *Mystery Girl.* But rules were rules and China seemed to have lots and lots of rules.

"Boy, are we ever going to get out of this airport?" grumbled Mimi. They had been through passport lines, immigration lines, and bathroom lines. Mimi was not fond of lines.

As they stood in line, Grant kept peeking at the map in his pocket. He was curious about the golden dragon with jade green curlicues all around it.

"What are you looking at?" Christina startled him by saying.

"Oh, nothing," said Grant, secretively. He just smiled and stuffed the map back in his pocket. He heard the dry parchment crinkle and hoped he hadn't torn the map.

"Confucius say...he who watches pot will never see water boil," said Papa in a silly voice.

"He did not!" argued Mimi with a giggle.

"Who is Confusion?" asked Grant.

"*Confucius,*" corrected Papa. "He was a famous Chinese philosopher who had helpful reminders in the form of special sayings."

"Papa?" said Grant.

"Yes," said Papa.

"That sounds just like you!" Grant said with a loud sigh. "You always have special reminders that you say loud and clear to kids."

Papa howled with laughter, attracting attention from the surrounding crowd.

Mimi gave Papa the Evil Eye, as Grant and Christina called it. "And Mimi always has Special Reminders for me, doesn't she?" Papa teased in a quieter voice and his grandchildren laughed.

Suddenly, they found that they had passed all the international traveler hurdles and were free to leave the airport. As they waited for a taxi, Christina asked, "Just how big is the country of China?"

Papa pretended to count on an "air" abacus, his fingers flying. "Let's see: China is so big it covers 50 degrees of latitude. It includes almost four million square miles. It is bordered by 14 different countries. It has a coastline more than 12,000 miles long. And, 20 percent of the people in the world live here."

"Wow!" said Grant. "How did you know all that?"

Papa nodded at a poster on a nearby wall. "I read it right there!"

"And Beijing is the capital," said Christina. "Where our pen pals live. I love getting postcards from them with neat stamps."

"Yes," said Papa. "Your pen pals and more than a billion of their friends live in China!"

Grant and Christina were quiet with awe at the massive numbers their grandfather tossed around, as a taxi van pulled up. However, when the taxi doors slid open, both kids began to squeal.

"Li!" screamed Christina.

"Cong!" shouted Grant.

"We would know you anywhere!" said Christina to their Chinese pen pals. For a year they had shared letters, postcards, emails, and photographs.

"Welcome to China!" Li and Cong cried together. "Land of Mystery!" they hinted in a line they had rehearsed just for this most auspicious meeting.

As they drove off, no one noticed the man frantically searching his pockets for a very important map that he had lost on the airplane.

Pen Pals

As they drove from the airport into Beijing, the kids chatted merrily in the back seat of the van. It was still very early in the morning, but the city was already **bustling**. Christina was only half listening, as she **marveled** at the old/new combinations she saw along the way: soaring skyscrapers...water buffalo pulling a plow in a field...lazy lakes with red-sailed boats called junks...a rush hour traffic jam...people in red silk dresses with dragon designs...and others in serious black business suits. It was amazing!

"Christina!" Li said, to get the daydreaming girl's attention.

"Sorry, Li," Christina mumbled, turning away from the window to look at her favorite pen pal. Li was petite with glistening black hair and eyes. She was an outstanding student. And, she loved the stuffed animal that Christina had brought her—a funny brown bloodhound that looked just like their dog, Clue, who was back home.

Li whispered, "Grant says that you have found a mysterious treasure map?"

Christina shook her head. "Grant says that he found a map, but I have not seen it. He keeps it hidden in his pocket. I think maybe he is teasing me. You know how little brothers are," Christina added.

Both Grant and Cong gave the girls the Evil Eye. The boys were playing with a video game that Grant had brought Cong as a gift. "It was hard to know what to get you," said Grant. "After all, everything in the whole wide world is made in your country."

"What's that?" asked Papa from the front seat.

"You know," said Grant. "All those tags on everything in America that say MADE IN CHINA."

Mimi and Papa laughed.

"We have gifts for you, too!" said Li, pulling a package from her purple backpack. She handed it to Christina.

Christina tore into the wrapping and pulled out a stuffed Panda bear. "Oh, that's perfect!" she cried. "I love Pandas and I know that they only live in China."

"And eat bamboo," added Li.

"And look like big, furry Oreo Cookies," said Grant.

Cong laughed. "I love Oreos. But here, Grant, I got you something just as tasty." He handed Grant a package.

When Grant opened his gift, he discovered a large bag of fortune cookies. "Hey, I know these Chinese Fortune Cookies were made in China!"

Papa laughed. "They might have been made here, but fortune cookies were invented in the United States."

"Well, I wish us all good *joss*...good fortune on this special trip," said Mimi.

"And I wish us lots of mystery!" said Grant.

"And why would you do that?" asked Mimi.

Grant put his hand in his pocket. "Oh, I just have this feeling..."

Christina interrupted her brother as they drove into downtown Beijing. "What is that?!" she asked. "And that?! And that?!"

Mimi laughed. "That's the famous Tian'an Men Square. It's where the People's Republic of China was founded." She waved her arm at the enormous open space surrounded by red and gold-frosted gates and filled with gawking tourists from around the world.

"And that's the famous Forbidden City," said Papa. "It's where 24 emperors ruled for almost 500 years." Everyone stared at the gigantic complex of orange-roofed palaces and other structures.

Forbidden, thought Grant. *That means I really want to go there!*

"And that," said Grant, to answer Christina's last question, "is a gazillion million bicycles." Indeed, the army of bikes spinning through the city seemed endless and amazing.

Suddenly, the taxi driver began to speak in a loud voice. He waved his arms around.

Li explained, "He's speaking Mandarin. He says this is your hotel."

"Hey, the sign says MARCO POLO," said Grant. "I know him!"

"You do?" asked Cong, surprised.

"Sure," said Grant. "He must have invented swimming pools, because every time we swim in Mimi's and Papa's pool, we play a game where we say *MARCO...POLO... MARCO...POLO... MARCO...POLO...*"

"Enough, Grant, please!" said Mimi. "Marco Polo traveled the famous Silk Road through China, in search of spices and silk...and other treasures."

As they got out of the taxi to go into the hotel, Grant pulled Christina aside. "Did you hear what Mimi said? She said treasure!"

"Well she also said, *no mystery, please,*" said Christina.

Grant frowned and shook his new bag of cookies. "Well, we'll just see what the fortune cookies say about that!"

One Hump, or Two?

As they checked into the hotel, the kids did not realize that they had been followed. The man at the airport who had been so frantic about his lost treasure map had been aboard their Air China flight. He had changed seats early in the boarding process, and later realized it was probable that one member of the family who had just arrived at the Marco Polo had been sitting in the seat he had previously occupied.

I'd almost bet it was that American boy, he thought to himself. *If he has my map, I wonder where it might be?*

As Grant waited for Papa to check in, he laid his bag of fortune cookies on a nearby table.

Then he and Cong took a tour of the lobby. When Papa called them back, Grant forgot about his gift. *It did not matter; it was no longer there.*

"You folks almost need a Bactrian camel to handle all your luggage!" said the porter. He tugged an overfilled luggage cart toward the elevator.

"What kind of camel is that?" asked Grant, as they boarded the elevator.

"The kind with two humps, not one," explained the porter. "Some of these creatures still live in the deserts of China."

"You have deserts in China?" asked Christina.

The porter laughed. "Deserts, jungles, bamboo forests, snowy mountain plateaus, grasslands, wetlands, seacoasts—we have it all!"

"You certainly speak very good English," Mimi noted.

"I am a student at a university in America. Beijing is my home. When I'm here, I work at the Marco Polo," the porter explained. "My name is John. I'll bet this is your first trip to China?" he guessed.

"It sure is," said Grant, "and we are in search of mystery!"

The porter laughed again. "Then you came to the right place!"

Before the kids could ask him what that meant, the elevator door opened and they all hurried to their rooms, which each had a lovely Chinese design.

"Very exotic!" said Mimi, pleased.

"Very expensive," grumbled Papa under his breath.

"Very cool!" said Christina and Grant as they learned that Li and Cong were going to stay with them a few days while their parents were away on a business trip.

"They are in import and export," Papa explained.

"It was so hard not to tell you this surprise!" said Li.

"That's one reason there's so much luggage," said Cong. "They were holding our suitcases behind the desk for our arrival."

The girls would be in one room; the boys in an adjoining room. What they never noticed was that checking into the room next to them was the man from the airport. And he looked as angry as a spitting camel!

A Treasure Map

After they had unpacked and gone downstairs to the restaurant to have tea, Grant passed the sugar bowl. "One hump or two?" he asked his grandmother with a giggle.

The kids sipped on tall glasses of lemonade with skinny red straws and little purple umbrellas. Each came with a fortune cookie.

When Mimi and Papa went back to the lobby to see about hiring a car, the kids opened their fortune cookies.

"Mine says: *Luck will follow you always,*" said Christina.

"Mine says: *You will travel a great distance,*" Li read.

"*You will go far in life,*" read Cong.

Grant was the last to get his cookie out of the plastic wrapper. He cracked the cookie open and pulled out a little slip of paper and read it.

"Well, what does it say, Grant?" asked Christina. "Is it a secret?"

Slowly, Grant shook his head. No," he answered, "it's a puzzle." Then he read aloud, his voice quivering just a little. *"Return my treasure map...OR ELSE!"*

"Grant!" said Christina. "You didn't really find a treasure map, did you?"

Her brother ducked his head and dug in his pocket. "See what you think," he said, as he spread the parchment out before them.

The children stared at the curious map. The golden dragon with the green curlicues around it looked ominous. Fire spewed from its mouth. There was a lot of Chinese writing all around the map. A large X was marked along what looked like a section of the Great Wall of China.

"Wow!" said Christina. "I thought you were just kidding."

"This is so mysterious," said Cong. "I never find treasure maps when I fly on airplanes...or go anywhere else. You are so lucky, Grant."

Grant did not look like he felt lucky. He looked like he wished that he had never found the map. "I sure don't know how to return it," he said. "Because I have no idea who it belongs to."

Li shook her head. "This is bad *joss*," she said. "I know Cong and I want to be in one of your grandmother's mystery books...but we want it to be a *pretend* mystery, not a *real* one. Especially a *dangerous* one."

"Dangerous?" said Christina. She felt goosebumps pimple up along her arms. "What do you mean?"

Li pointed to the fortune cookie note. "What do you think OR ELSE means?" she asked. "It can't mean anything good. It sounds like a serious threat to me."

"Maybe if we find the treasure, we can return the treasure instead of the map?" Cong suggested.

Grant looked shocked. "If I find any treasure, I'm sure not returning it! Finders, keepers, losers, weepers."

Christina giggled. "Did Confucius say that?"

Grant folded his arms over his chest and frowned. "No, I said it. How do we even know the treasure belongs to this person? Or even that the map does? In fact, these actually look like my fortune cookies from Cong. Maybe they were stolen from me. I say we look for the treasure."

"Well, that will be hard," said Christina, "since we can't read the map." She ran her finger under one line of the curious writing as if trying to read it.

Li and Cong giggled. "That's not the right way," said Li. "Chinese is read from right to left."

Cong looked at the map. "This is Pinyin, a real simplified form of Chinese writing, like we use in school."

Christina stared at the pretty black symbols. "It might as well be Greek to me."

"So maybe this map is not so old?" asked Grant.

"I don't think so," said Li.

"Good!" said Grant. "Then this is *fresh* treasure, not some old stuff buried deep for centuries. That should make it easier to find."

"Oh, Grant," said Christina. "You are such an optimist."

"Yes, he has good *yang*," Li said.

Grant grinned as he put the map back in his pocket. "Confucius say he who positive finds treasure."

"Or trouble," said Li.

Suddenly, Papa appeared behind them. "Come on, you guys," he said. "Your chariot awaits!"

A Ride in a Rickshaw

Outside, the children were delighted that instead of a car, Papa had hired rickshaws for the afternoon—three red rickshaws with red and white bench seats and fringed tops. Three men in red suits and caps stood ready to bike them around Beijing.

"What fun!" said Christina as she and Li climbed in one rickshaw. The boys piled in the second, and Mimi and Papa into the third. Papa said something to the driver and off they went!

Christina was amazed by the sights and sounds and smells. They passed a big, gold, laughing Buddha. A policeman directed traffic from a round, red and white striped stand. A multi-storied gold-topped pagoda glistened in the sunlight.

"I wonder where we're going?" said

Christina over the loud street noise. She turned and waved at the boys who waved back. B e h i n d them Papa was oogling all the sights. Mimi held tightly to the side of her rickshaw.

Suddenly, there was a burst of noise. It startled Christina and Grant, but Li and Cong just laughed.

"It's fireworks!" Li explained. "This is Spring Festival...what you probably call Chinese New Year. It's the Year of the Dog. There will be lots of parades and fireworks."

No sooner had Li said this when their rickshaws were blocked by a passing parade. Papa hopped out of his rickshaw and came over. "Well, we might as well stop and enjoy the parade," he said.

The kids cheered and hopped out of their rickshaws to stand together at the edge of the street. The noisy parade was a colorful affair of hot pink, orange, gold, lime, yellow, red, and turquoise blue.

"Hey, Christina, look!" Grant said as he nudged his sister with an elbow, "Here there be dragons!"

Long, snake-like, two-headed dragons slithered by. A band of drummers, wearing bright red and gold uniforms, marched between the brightly-colored serpents.

"The noise is supposed to keep away evil spirits," Li explained.

Christina thought how often the ideas of good and evil, good luck or bad, positive and negative came up in Chinese conversation. She thought that superstition must play a powerful role in Chinese society. Then she thought of how she and Grant squealed when a black cat crossed their path back at home, and how they refused to walk under a ladder.

Cong pulled a pretty red envelope from his pocket. "We got our *hongbao* earlier," he said.

"You got what!?" Grant exclaimed. A *hongbao* didn't sound good. Then he saw the envelope. "What is it?"

"Money!" said Cong. "It is given to kids, sort of like your Christmas presents."

"So are tangerines!" squealed Li, as a passing parader tossed them each a bright, orange fruit for "good luck." All except Grant, who received another wrapped fortune cookie.

"Hey, no fair!" said Grant. Then he realized what he probably had: another clue! He stuck it in his pocket to open later. *But he shouldn't have waited.*

Face to Face with a Dragon!

As the dramatic parade continued, the kids munched on mooncakes that Papa bought them. A dragon boat sped by, followed by festive dancers and marching soldiers. More fireworks *POP–POP–POPPED.*

Soon, the end of the parade was in sight. Mimi and Papa climbed back in their rickshaw. So did Li and Christina. Grant and Cong still stood and watched an enormous dragon—made of colorful fabric with people beneath holding it up—sway back and forth across the street.

Suddenly, the dragon headed right for them. Much to their surprise, the dragon's head lifted up and Grant and Cong found themselves face to face with the angry man.

"Give me the map, boy!" he demanded. His jade green eyes glared at Grant's baby blue eyes. "NOW!" he screamed. Only the boys could hear him over the din of the parade noise and the crackling fireworks.

Before the boys could move or speak, the man thrust his face back beneath the dragon head as those behind him pressed him onward.

Grant and Cong looked at one another...and ran to jump in their rickshaw!

The Forbidden City

The three rickshaws took off at a fast pace, weaving through and around the parade-watchers returning to their homes, or schools, or work. Tourists hardly moved. They just stood there as if they could not believe what they had just seen.

Grant and Cong certainly could not believe what they had just seen. They did not know this man, but he seemed to know them. *How could that be? Was the map really his? Just how desperate was he to get it back? Why was he so angry? How could he know Grant had it?*

Grant had no answers, but suddenly he remembered something. As the rickshaw lurched left and right, he pulled the fortune cookie from his pocket. Quickly, he opened it. Out popped the fortune. It read:

I'll see you in the Forbidden City!

As the three rickshaws stopped side by side at a traffic light, Grant called over to his grandfather. "Papa, where are we going?"

Papa called back, "The Forbidden City. It's just ahead!"

A few minutes later they arrived at the large historic complex known as the Forbidden City.

As they waited for Papa to pay the rickshaw, Mimi explained:

"The Forbidden City was originally known as the Palace Museum. It's a monument to the 500 years during which China was ruled by 24 different dynasties." She waved her arm toward the endless array of walls and gates and buildings and courtyards—all topped in bright orange terracotta roof tiles.

"What's a dynasty?" asked Christina.

"A family whose members rule over a long period of time," said Mimi. "Each ruler was called an emperor."

"Each dynasty had a name," added Li. "Han, Tang, Shang, Yaun, Ming, Song, and names like that."

"We're going to see a short film soon," said Mimi. "You'll learn more about China's history."

"I hope it's short," said Christina. "I want to go explore."

"I hope it's long," said Grant.

"Why?" Mimi asked, surprised. No one liked to explore more than Grant.

Grant just shrugged his shoulders and hung his head. He did not want to admit that he was a little scared of this angry man. Maybe in a dark movie theater, the man could not find him.

Just then, Papa returned and steered his crew through an enormous gate and into the Forbidden City.

It seemed eerie to go inside the dark, cool movie theater after being out in the bright, noisy city. They all settled back to watch the short film about Chinese history.

Grant and Christina had sympathy for Li and Cong after learning that China's history dated back more than 10,000 years! That was a lot of facts to learn to pass tests in school, thought Christina.

The story of China was fascinating and confusing. There were a lot of wars. They were impressed by all the beautiful art the Chinese had made. The film showed tapestries, vases, and, of course, the Great Wall.

They were surprised to learn that the Chinese had invented the wheelbarrow, paper, the decimal system, printing, the magnetic compass, the seismometer to measure earthquakes, and gunpowder—the source of all those fireworks! They also invented the abacus, called the first computer.

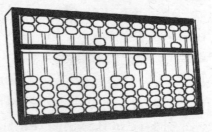

The Cultural Revolution seemed like a sad and terrible part of China's history. Christina didn't understand all the parts about Communism and was glad when they got to the part about modern China and its economic boom.

Just as the kids began to get bored, the movie ended. They walked back out into the bright sunshine, squinting.

"Christina! Li!" Grant hissed, as Mimi and Papa walked on ahead.

"What?" asked Christina, waiting up for the two boys.

As the kids huddled in a small knot, Grant told the girls how they had seen the angry man beneath the dragon costume. Grant then showed them the fortune cookie that said he would find them at the Forbidden City.

"Well, we'd better be on the lookout," said Christina. "What does he look like?"

Grant looked puzzled. "Like a Chinese man," he finally said in exasperation. "Like all these Chinese men!"

"I might recognize him," said Cong. "Did you notice the scar he had over his eyebrow? And when he pulled his dragon costume up, I saw a yellow silk lining in his suit coat."

"That's not much help," said Li.

"Let's stick close together and keep our eyes open," Christina suggested. "Maybe we should tell Mimi and Papa?"

"No!" pleaded Grant. "I want to find the treasure. And we have no proof this man has anything to do with it. Maybe he just saw me get it out of the pocket on the airplane. He just might want it for himself."

"That's possible," Christina admitted.

Before they could discuss the matter further, Papa waved for them to join them. Soon, they were exploring places with names like the Palace of Earthly Tranquility, Hall of Imperial Peace, and Nine Dragon Screen.

"What's with this dragon thing?" asked Grant. "It seems weird to have fire-breathing beasts all over the place."

Li frowned. "In China, we consider dragons magical. They protect, bring good luck, and ward off evil spirits."

"Can they ward off that evil spirit?" Christina whispered. As unobtrusively as she could, she pointed up to one of the palace walls. There stood a man in a black suit with a white shirt. He had his hand up to shield his eyes from the sun as he scanned the courtyards. His upraised arm caused his jacket to gape open so that they could see the yellow lining glint in the sunlight.

"It's good we're hidden behind this Nine Dragon Screen," said Cong.

"I told you dragons were good luck!" Li said.

"But we're not hidden from Papa," said Christina with a groan.

The kids looked and saw Papa waving for them to catch up with he and Mimi. Of course, to do that, they had to come out from behind the large panel of dragon art.

Walking as slowly as they could, the four children finally emerged from behind the wall. Grant was last and looked relieved when he saw that the man was gone from the top of the wall.

"You kids must be getting hungry!" said Mimi. "How about an early lunch?"

The kids nodded hungrily. Papa headed off toward a restaurant, saying, "Well, come then! *Wok* this way!"

The kids groaned at Papa's stir-fried humor, then eagerly followed him...*hoping no one was following them.*

The Hong Kong Express

Leaving the Forbidden City, Papa herded them into the first restaurant he saw, called the Hong Kong Express.

Everyone was happy to sit down in the cool air-conditioning and rest. The kids realized that they were, indeed, very hungry.

Instead of some old, formal Chinese style, this restaurant was funky and upbeat with lots of black leather, shiny silver chrome, and colorful neon lights.

"The menu's just about as big as I am," said Grant.

"Maybe it's the kids menu?" Papa teased, "if it's as big as a kid?"

The kids groaned. Papa was always making corny jokes. Mimi always laughed at them.

After they ordered, the kids asked if they could look around the display cases in the restaurant while they waited for their food to be served. Mingled with the modern décor were glass cases filled with what looked like ancient Chinese artifacts.

As they got up, Christina glanced at her brother. She noticed that he looked much more relaxed. Surely they were safe from the angry man here? But when would they ever really get to look for a treasure that seemed to be located somewhere on the Great Wall? Mimi and Papa had not even said anything about visiting that famous historic site yet. And besides, the Wall was thousands of miles long—good luck finding the location drawn on the map!

"Wow!" said Cong, looking at one of the larger display cases. "Look at the famous Terracotta Army!"

Grant and Christina stared at the large photo of the enormous army—more than 7,000 soldiers, the display said—all standing in what looked like an endless gravesite!

"What in the world?" asked Christina.

Li explained eagerly. "This amazing army made of clay was discovered by some Chinese workers digging a well. It turned out that an emperor ordered more than 700,000 people to work on his tomb. It took them at least 36 years to make this enormous army to **accompany** him to the afterlife."

Christina peered closely at the photos and the replica of one soldier. "They each have a different expression," she marveled, "and different hairstyles. It's amazing."

"And once they were each painted in bright colors," added Cong, pointing to another picture. "But that faded away over time and, as you can see, the wooden weapons they once held rotted away."

"If I was digging a well and saw this," said Grant, "I'd think I was dreaming!"

Suddenly, Grant grew very quiet. Christina could tell just by looking at her brother that he was upset.

"What is it, Grant?" she whispered, as Li and Cong continued to examine the Terracotta Army display.

Grant nodded toward a dark booth. "I think the man sitting there is looking at us," he said nervously.

Christina looked, but it was so dark in that booth that she could not really see anything but a shadow.

Suddenly the shadow stood up and came toward them. "It's OK, Grant," Christina said with a giggle. "False alarm!" With relief, both kids looked at the enormous man taking his bill to the counter to pay.

"Hey!" said Cong. "Do you know who that is?"

Christina looked puzzled. "Well, he's not our bad guy."

"Not unless he ate a whole bunch of lunch," added Grant.

Cong gave Grant a funny look. "No, it's not the bad guy," he said. "It's Hai Ku, a very famous Sumo wrestler."

"I'll bet he's here to work on the 2008 Olympics," said Li. "They will be held in Beijing, you know."

Grant beamed. In an Arnold Schwarzenegger voice he intoned, "Then I'LL BE BACK!"

The kids were all doubled over giggling, when a big gong went...

BOOOOOOOOOOOOOONG!

"I think that means our food is ready?" guessed Li.

"From the look on Papa's face, it's *been* ready," Christina warned them.

As they scampered to their table, they did not notice a second man emerge from the dark corner booth. He spoke with a waiter briefly, then pulled some *juan* from his jacket pocket, *a jacket lined in yellow silk.*

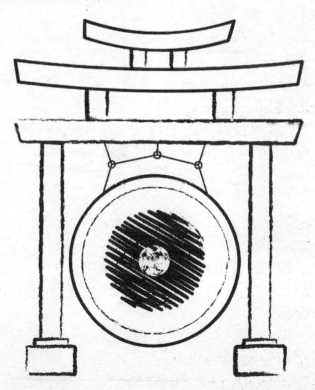

The "Flowerpot" Army

"Sorry," said Grant, as they quickly sat down. The waiter draped oversized red napkins across their laps. "We were looking at the flowerpot army."

"The what?" asked Papa.

"It's the Terracotta Army," Li corrected.

"Oh, yeah," said Grant. "I just know Mimi said her flowerpots are made of terracotta."

"Very good, Grant," said Mimi. "And I have an army of them, too, don't I?" she added.

Mimi loved flowers and the kids always had to worry that when they traveled, their grandmother would drag them to and through gardens instead of amusement parks, for example.

It happened every time. Christina hoped not this time—it was time they headed to the Great Wall with their treasure map! She was getting as anxious as Grant to solve this mystery and get some distance between them and the angry man.

"This is lunch!?" Christina exclaimed. Before them was an array of food like she had never seen before.

Li pointed to each dish as she named them: "Mongolian Hotpot (sort of like your fondu), Mu Shu Pork, Prawns (big shrimp), and..."

Grant interrupted her. "I know those," he said, pointing to a long stick that pierced enough apples for each of them. "Candied apples!"

Everyone laughed and began to eat. This time, when tea was poured in a long arc into their cups, they hardly noticed. In fact, they hardly noticed anything but the delicious food on their plates disappearing. That is, until Papa served the candied apple dessert.

"Oops," he said, "It seems we're short one apple."

"It is OK, sir!" said a waiter who suddenly appeared. "A guest ordered this especially for the young gentleman's dessert today." Everyone looked surprised as Grant was presented with a large red plate with an unwrapped fortune cookie sitting in the center of it.

Everyone laughed except Grant and Christina. "Maybe the Sumo wrestler sent it over," said Cong.

"Maybe a secret admirer," Li teased.

Grant didn't smile. Mistaking Grant's seriousness for disappointment, Papa said, "I'll be glad to let you have my candied apple. I like my apples baked in a pie, anyway." He poked his apple with a chopstick and placed it on Grant's plate, right next to the ominous fortune cookie.

Mimi laid her red napkin beside her plate. "While you kids enjoy your dessert, I think Papa and I will go take a look at the Flowerpot Army!"

When she and Papa left the table, the kids urged Grant to open the fortune cookie clue and read the note inside. It said:

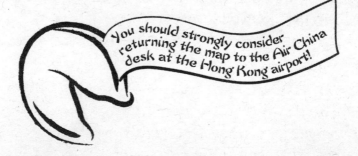

You should strongly consider returning the map to the Air China desk at the Hong Kong airport!

Grant surprised the kids by laughing out loud. "Well, that makes me feel better," he said.

"Why?" asked Cong. "It still sounds like a threat to me."

"I think Grant means that we are not going to Hong Kong, so he can't return the map," Christina explained, looking at Grant who nodded.

"Ahhh..." said Li, "so...the man must have an appointment or something and has to go to Hong Kong...which means he will be leaving Beijing?"

"Leaving us alone!" said Grant, hopefully.

He was still grinning and crunching cookie and apple together when Mimi and Papa returned to the table.

"Guess what, kids?" Papa said. "Guess where we're going?" Papa was so excited he couldn't wait for their guess, so he told them: "To HONG KONG!"

Hung Up in Hong Kong

The four kids were momentarily speechless, until Grant blurted out, "Hong Kong!? Phooey!"

"That's where Mom and Dad are!" Li and Cong exclaimed.

"They'll be so excited to meet y'all!" Cong said, imitating a Southern accent.

"How did you decide this so quickly?" Christina asked, confused.

"When you kids were looking around the restaurant, I thought you should see the real Hong Kong," Mimi explained.

"But Hong Kong is where..." Grant began, then stopped. He looked like he might sob.

"Is where what?" Papa asked, surprised to see his grandson look so disappointed.

"Uh, is where the Great Wall *isn't...*" said Grant.

Papa laughed. "Oh, we'll get to the Great Wall, I promise," he said. "But a detour to exciting Hong Kong won't hurt us, will it?"

The four children did not answer because they really weren't so sure about that.

Within the hour, the group had returned to the Marco Polo, quickly packed their overnight bags, and were headed to the airport. They would be in Hong Kong in time for dinner, Papa said.

"And," said Mimi, "you won't even miss the fireworks."

The children were puzzled by this remark, but they were too busy powwowing in the back seat of the taxi to wonder what Mimi meant.

"How do you think this happened?" Christina whispered urgently to the other kids.

"I'll bet the mean man was in the restaurant," said Li. "I'll bet he overheard your grandparents discussing a trip to Hong Kong. Then he paid a waiter to deliver that fortune cookie to Grant...and he knew just what message to write!"

"So this bad guy could be aboard the very Air China flight we are taking?" guessed Cong.

"Hey, wait a minute," said Christina. "You know, we keep assuming this guy is a bad guy. Maybe he's not at all. Maybe he's afraid we will try to look for treasure in some dangerous place. Or get in trouble if we find it. Maybe he is trying to protect us."

"We should be open to all ideas," Li agreed.

"But I don't think this idea is the right one," argued Cong.

Suddenly, Papa twisted around from the front seat of the taxi. "What are you kids mumbling about back there? Any problems?"

"No, sir," the four kids promised. Christina peeked and saw that each of them had their fingers crossed behind their backs!

"Just looking forward to good, old King Kong," said Grant.

Mimi giggled. "It's Hong Kong, Grant. You know that," she said.

"Oh, I don't know," said Grant. "You just never know when some big gorilla is going to jump out and get you, do you?"

The other kids gave Grant a worried look, but Mimi and Papa ignored their grandson's remark. The taxi had pulled up to the airport and they had to hurry to catch their flight in time.

In the taxi behind them, a man in a black suit grabbed his own overnight bag. With an evil grin on his face, he jumped out of his taxi and tipped the driver and ran...for the same Air China flight to good, old Hong Kong.

Somewhere Over China

Settled in aboard the airplane, the four friends tried to relax and enjoy themselves. It was so much fun to get to know pen pals that you had corresponded with for so long, Christina thought. She knew that people from different countries often had different backgrounds, different politics, different religions, and different cultures. But to Christina, Li and Cong seemed to be just like her and Grant—kids who liked to joke, tease, have fun, learn new things, play, and see new sights.

"Hong Kong is where many of my mystery books are printed," Mimi explained to the children, once they were in the air and free to move about the cabin. "The Chinese have a wonderful eye for color and a long history in printing beautiful books."

"How do the books get back to America?" asked Grant.

"You know those big ships filled with gigantic metal containers we see when we go to the port in Savannah?" asked Papa.

Grant nodded.

"That's how the goods are delivered—in those containers. Then they are taken off the ship and put on trains or trucks and make their way to their destination," Papa explained. "It takes a while!" he added.

"So have you thought of an idea for a mystery set in China?" Li politely asked Mimi.

Mimi smiled. "No," she admitted. "We have just been too busy, don't you think?"

Cong piped up. "We could help you with an idea!" he insisted. "I am sure we could give you a really good idea for a mystery, with a bad guy and treasure and everything—"

Cong did not get to finish his sentence. Grant accidentally (on purpose) tipped his cup of tea into his friend's lap. "Oh, sorry, sorry, sorry, Cong!" Grant exclaimed. Mimi handed Cong a handful of napkins to wipe up the mess.

"Gee, thanks, Grant," said Cong. "Now it looks like I wet my pants!"

Christina and Li giggled, but they were glad that Grant had figured out some way to hush Cong up before he said too much.

Suddenly, the airplane jerked up and down. The captain announced that everyone should return to their seats and fasten their seatbelts. Mimi scooted back to her seat beside Papa, across the aisle from the children.

"Grant! Why did you do that?" Cong hissed as the airplane jolted them again.

"You can't tell about the treasure map, Cong," Grant begged. "Just be patient and I promise that you will end up in a Mimi mystery."

"But she says that she does not have a mystery," said Li.

Christina grinned. "You don't know our grandmother like we do," she said. "Just when you least expect it..."

Now it was Christina who did not get to complete her sentence. Everyone had returned to their seats after the captain's announcement, except for one man who had been in the lavatory at the front of the plane.

The restroom door suddenly flew open and banged loudly against the wall, startling some of the passengers. The man staggered down the aisle, grabbing one seat, then another as he passed, trying to keep his balance in the turbulence that bounced the plane through the air.

The children had no doubt that he was their treasure map guy. His eyes were jade green. His suit was black. His shirt was white. And every time he grabbed a seat, his jacket flipped open to reveal a yellow lining.

If they'd had any doubt at all, it was immediately dispelled when the man passed their row. Even though the airplane was stable at that moment, he still bolted to one side. As he hovered over their seats, he held his fist near Grant's face, then opened his hand and let an object fall into Grant's lap. Then he hurried on down the aisle to his seat in the rear of the plane.

The man had been blocking Mimi's and Papa's view, so they never saw a thing. Grant looked down, feeling sure he knew what the object was—a fortune cookie.

As the other kids held up magazines and other objects that they pretended to read or look at, Grant tore the wrapper off the cookie. His hands trembled as he pulled out the note. He pulled down his tray table and spread out the note. The other kids huddled as close as they

could as Grant read as loudly as he dared:

"Are you going to leave the map there, Grant?" Li asked. She looked very worried, like that might be the best idea.

"Of course he is!" said Cong. "Just how many 'or elses' can we take?!"

Christina was quiet. She knew her brother better than that. She knew that he was sweet and smart and silly and sometimes quiet. Like now. He was thinking, but she already knew what he would say, because she would say the same thing.

"No!" said Grant. "It's my map till someone tells me otherwise. I just can't let someone intimidate me. If that guy really thought this was his map, he would not pester little kids like us—he would go right to Mimi and Papa."

It was clear that Grant had made up his mind. At least, Christina thought, they were near the front of the plane and the bad guy was near the back. They would be off and long gone before he got off, she hoped. And, when they got to Hong Kong, maybe Li's and Cong's parents would add extra protection...four kids, four adults. *Good luck, bad guy,* she thought.

Before long the pilot announced that they were on approach for landing. The kids felt prepared for their quick exit from the airplane. However, they were not prepared for the sight of Hong Kong and its lovely Victoria Harbor. As the airplane banked to one side to line up with the runway, the four kids could clearly see the jigsaw puzzle of green islands in the blue sea.

"Wow!" said Christina. "What a pretty sight."

"Yeah," said Grant, "look at that mountain!"

Li and Cong were speechless. At last Li

spoke. "Our parents come here all the time on business. They buy things in Hong Kong and export them to other countries. But Cong and I have never been to Hong Kong."

Cong was silent. He did not look happy. He looked at Grant and frowned. "I still think it's a good idea to return the map," he said under his breath. "Or else, Grant," he added. "The man said, OR ELSE!"

Let the Fireworks Begin!

As the plane came in for a landing, the kids continued to marvel at the sight of magical Hong Kong beneath them. Papa pointed and named places: "Victoria Harbor, Kowloon, Macau, New Territories, Chicken Chow Mein..."

"Papa!" said Christina. "You are so silly."

Her grandfather just gave her a puzzled look. "Me no speak English," he insisted, and the kids giggled. But as Papa turned his attention to other things, the kids grew serious. The plane had landed and was now taxiing toward the terminal. They knew that in just a moment, it would be a race to beat the man off of the plane, through the terminal, and away toward the city before he could manage to follow them.

As soon as the bell *dinged* that they could release their seat belts, the four kids jumped up, grabbed their backpacks, and headed down the aisle toward the door. Most of the adults moved so slowly or had so much luggage to get out of the overhead compartments, that the kids easily were among the first few people off the plane.

Grant, who had been last in line, had given Mimi and Papa a quick wave and pointed toward the terminal. He figured they would know he meant "meet you at baggage claim." But once the kids raced through the airport to the baggage claim carousels, they found that all their haste had been a waste. They just stood there and waited on Mimi, Papa, the luggage to appear...and the man.

"Oh, no! I forgot!" Christina cried suddenly. "Mimi and Papa just have an overnight bag with them in the overhead bin...we don't need to be here at the baggage claim."

Li looked all around the throng of people gathering to claim their luggage. "Well, I guess the bad guy didn't have luggage either. I don't see him anywhere."

"Good!" said Grant, looking around, too. "Then let's get out of here in case he shows up."

Pulling their wheeled backpacks, the kids hurried on through the airport. Suddenly, Christina, who was leading the way, stopped. Li, who was next, bumped into her. Cong bumped into them. Grant fell on top of Cong.

"What is it?" Grant asked, pulling himself up.

Christina pointed ahead. "We have to walk past the Air China counter to get to the exit."

"Uh, oh," said Li. She nodded. In a small crowd of people near the center of the long counter, stood the angry man. He was looking all around, but could not see them through the crowd.

"This is your chance," Cong pleaded with Grant. "To turn the map in."

"No way," said Grant. "I have an idea. Everyone follow me—hurry!"

Quick as a firecracker, Grant popped behind the counter where the busy agents were working. The other kids followed closely behind, stooping down so as not to be seen from the front of the counter.

As they passed behind each agent, the agents either grumbled, gave them a warning look, or ignored them. Soon they reached the end of the counter. Grant peeked out and could see the man looking for them in the wrong direction. "Come on!" he said, and dashed for the exit door.

Before the man ever turned around, the kids were out the door. They spied Mimi and Papa at the taxi stand looking all around for them. The kids waved and dashed to catch up. By the time they got to the taxi stand, Papa had the taxi doors open and the kids jumped in.

"I was starting to worry where you kids were," said Mimi, as she settled down in the jump seat.

"We're so used to having sooo many bags we went to the baggage claim," Christina explained. She left off the part about taking a detour behind the ticket counter.

"But why are you kids slumped down in your seats like that?" asked Papa, as he got in and slammed the door behind him.

"Uh," Grant began. "I guess we're just tired?"

Slowly and deliberately, the kids sat up straight. They figured that they had gotten far enough away from the terminal that the man could never see them now. However, as the taxi sped toward downtown Hong Kong, the kids looked out the window just in time to see another taxi race past them. They could see the man through the back window. He glared at them with an evil grin...and waved a firecracker threateningly toward each of them in turn.

Victoria Peak

"Then you'll be too tired to see the fireworks show, I guess?" Mimi asked.

The kids finally looked her way. "What fireworks?" Christina asked.

"Oh, we know!" said Li and Cong together.

"Our parents told us," Li explained. "Every night there is a big fireworks show over Victoria Harbor. The best place to see it is from Victoria Peak."

"Where's that?" asked Christina. It was turning dusk and the sun was setting.

"Right up there!" Papa said. The kids could see the green mountain looming before them, half of it draped in shadow.

Suddenly, the taxi stopped. "Please take our bags on to the hotel," Papa said.

"We're getting out here?" asked Grant, "Isn't this the bottom of the mountain?"

"Yes," said Mimi, "but the Peak Tram will take us up in just a few minutes!"

The kids hopped out of the taxi and looked. The Peak Tram was a small train. A very steep track spiked up toward the top of the mountain.

"It's called a funicular railway," Papa said as they climbed aboard. "It doesn't have an engine; it operates on a cable that pulls it up."

At first, the trip was fun and exciting. But it grew scary and scarier as they scaled the steep-sided mountain.

"Once upon a time, rich people paid Chinese workers to haul them, in sedan chairs, up the mountain to their expensive homes," Mimi explained. "The only way to get anything up the mountain—food, building materials, furniture—was to lug it up by hand."

The kids stared. They couldn't imagine that. They also couldn't imagine that they were climbing so high in the sky. Just as they reached the top of the mountain, the first firecracker went off! They hurried to a good place to view the harbor below and watched the spectacular light show!

Grant and Christina thought that they had never seen so many firecrackers in their lives.   *RED... BLUE...*

BLAM!

GREEN... WHITE... GOLD... PURPLE... RED BLUE AND GREEN... WHITE AND SILVER... GREEN AND GOLD...

POPP!

BLAM!   CRACK! CRAAAAAAAACK! BLAMMMMMMM! POPPP!

There were firecrackers going off constantly...one on top of the other...one behind another... left, right, up, down...it was a blast of brilliant color like a kaleidoscope in the sky!

GREEN

"Wow!" cried Grant above the din.   "This is the best fireworks show I have ever seen."

"It's as if the fireworks factory exploded!" Christina agreed.

"That happens sometimes," Papa admitted.

"Oh, look!" said Mimi and they all stared at the spectacular finale that ended the show with a deafening *BANG*,

CRACK!

leaving only the smell of sulphur.

and an enormous, wispy cloud of white smoke against the black sky.

"Oh, thank you for bringing us up here," said Christina. "I thought Hong Kong might be boring."

"I'd say we got started off with a bang!" said Grant.

"Can we walk back down the mountain?" asked Li.

"Well," said Papa, "our hotel *is* at the bottom of the mountain."

"Oh, please!" the kids cried together.

"I could use a little more fresh air after being in an airplane all afternoon," said Mimi. She and Papa looked around and saw that some other people were heading toward paths that wound down the mountain.

"OK," said Papa. "But it's dark. Stay together and stay in front of us! Every time you follow us, we adults seem to get left behind."

The kids nodded in agreement and set off down the path Mimi pointed toward— Governor's Walk, a sign read.

At first, the four kids walked arm in arm, admiring the neon lights and brightly lit ferry boats in the harbor below. Every now and then, they glanced back to see Mimi and Papa following closely behind them.

However, as the path grew more steep and narrow, they first divided into twosomes, then single-file as the path became more overgrown. The farther they walked, the more overgrown the path became. And slippery. And darker. When the kids turned to check on Mimi and Papa, they could no longer see them.

"I'll bet Mimi had to slow up on this slippery path," said Christina. "Maybe we should slow up and wait on them."

"I'm trying," Grant insisted. "But I'm having a gravity attack!"

"A what?" asked Cong, breathless.

"Gravity is pulling me faster and faster down the mountain," said Grant, speeding on ahead of them.

"Don't be silly, Grant," said Christina.

"Be careful, Grant," added Li. "You will fall. Wait for us."

But Grant continued to bolt down the path. As the other kids raced to catch up, Christina grabbed her flashlight from her backpack. When they turned the next corner,

she heard a scream and looked up just in time
to see Grant vanish!

Vanished!

"Oh, no!" cried Li. "I think Grant just fell off the mountain!"

The kids raced to the place where they had seen Grant tumble into the bushes. Suddenly, just as quickly as he had disappeared, Grant tumbled back out of the bushes and onto the path. He looked rumpled and shaken.

"Grant!" Christina cried. "Are you OK? What happened?"

At first, Grant could not speak. Finally, he said, "I got shanghaied! Someone grabbed me! They pulled me off the path. Next, they shook me up a little, like a Chinese milkshake, then shoved me back on the path." He looked confused and scared. All of a sudden, a look of awareness crossed his face.

Grant surprised the other kids by grabbing at his clothes, which were twisted this way and that. When he finally found his jacket pocket and began to check it, the kids realized what he was looking for. They held their breaths until he pulled out the treasure map...and a fortune cookie!

"Whew!" said Grant. "At least he didn't get the map!"

"Did he get anything?" asked his sister.

Grant grinned. "Yeah. I also had an old Chinese restaurant take-out menu in that pocket...I guess he got that."

"Whoa!" said Cong. "That is going to be one mad bad guy when he figures that out."

"Yes!" said Li. "We'd better get out of here before he finds out and comes back for you."

But all that was solved when the kids heard Papa calling. "Come on back!" he yelled. "This is too slippery and dark; we're going to take the tram back."

Eagerly, the kids began to run back up the mountain path. Huffing and puffing, they had almost caught up with Mimi and Papa when Christina pulled her brother aside.

"What is it?" he asked, surprised.

"Don't you want to read the new clue?" she asked in exasperation.

"The what?"

"The clue! The fortune cookie!"

"Oh, yeah," Grant said. He opened his hand. He had held the cookie so tightly that it was now so crushed to bits so that it was easy to read the little paper. Christina shined her flashlight on the note and read:

"I just wish that were a fortune that would come true," said Christina, "that he would leave us alone."

"Christina! Grant!" Papa hollered.

Grant stuck the cookie in a pocket. Christina turned off her flashlight and they made one last dash to catch up with the others. Quickly they all hurried to catch the last tram ride down for the night.

It was even scarier going down, watching the mountain disappear behind them as the ground rushed up to meet them. When they finally got to the bottom of Victoria Peak and climbed off the train, the kids were more than eager to get into the waiting taxi. So eager, that they never saw the man suddenly emerge from the bushes onto the street and shake his fist at them as the taxi sped away!

Star Ferry

Later, the kids were surprised to see the taxi pull up to the Star Ferry terminal.

"Wow! We must be going to stay up all night," said Grant. Hong Kong seemed to be in full swing. The enormous green and white ferry boat was crowded with passengers.

"We thought we'd go to Kowloon for dinner," said Mimi.

"Dinner, that sounds good," said Cong, rubbing his tummy.

The ferry pulled away from the dock just moments after they boarded. There was no sign of the mean man who had grabbed Grant on the mountain. The kids cheered and scampered to find a good place at the rail to wave goodbye to the city of Hong Kong, lit up so brightly that it looked much like a gigantic amusement park midway.

When Hong Kong grew smaller as they headed out into the harbor, the kids turned their attention to the city of Kowloon, coming more clearly into view. Soon, they approached that dock and the kids hurried to be first to get off.

Christina and Grant were surprised when Li and Cong began to cry and scream and wave and jump up and down.

"It's our parents!" cried Li. "They are here to greet us!"

As soon as they were allowed, Li and Cong ran off the ferry and into the arms of their waiting parents. When the others caught up, everyone was introduced and Mr. Fu announced that they were taking everyone to their favorite restaurant. It was on a large boat docked on the water.

The adults walked on ahead and the kids followed, arm in arm.

"This is so much fun," said Christina, "to be out so late at night in a glamorous international city, going to dinner on a big boat."

"Yeah," said Grant, "especially since I feel pretty sure we could not have been followed this time. I'll bet our nemesis, Mr. Meanie, is already at home in his pajamas...ordering Chinese take-out...from my menu!"

All the other kids laughed, except Cong. "Let's hope so," he said quietly.

Aboard the boat, the children were delighted at the long buffet of food. "It looks like a real banquet!" said Papa, with delight.

Little cards beside each dish told what it was: pickled vegetables; 10,000-year-old eggs; seasoned jellyfish.

"Well, I *was* hungry," said Grant, disgusted at the thought of eating eggs that had been around that long! "I wouldn't eat that for all the tea in China..."

"It's good manners to try a little of everything," hinted Mrs. Fu, as the children took their plates.

"Oh, OK," said Grant, helping himself to some fried scorpion!

Soon they were all settled at a table. As their host, Mr. Fu asked about their travels so far and if they were enjoying China.

Then Papa asked the Fus, "Tell us about your business; it sounds very interesting."

Mr. Fu smiled. "It keeps us very busy. We buy quality jade and export it to major museum gift shops around the world."

"Jade has been carved and polished by the Chinese for thousands of years," Mrs. Fu explained.

"However," said Mr. Fu with a frown, "the local news here is full of a scandalous story of a jade thief in China. Somehow, he is stealing some of the most prized pieces that should be going to museums. No one knows who he is or how he is getting away with this. It has upset the jade market tremendously."

Christina wasn't sure of Chinese etiquette, but she thought it was OK for kids to talk at dinner, so she asked, "So...when you say jade, you mean that pretty green stone? Mimi has a jade chess set."

Mr. Fu nodded. "But jade can also come in brown or black, and most especially prized is white."

Mrs. Fu reached into her purse and pulled out two small jade animals and put them on the table. They were very green.

"Those are beautiful!" said Christina. She touched one piece with her finger and it felt smooth and cool.

"You may have these as our way to say welcome to our country," said Mrs. Fu. She offered the jade panda to Grant and the jade  elephant to Christina. "Jade is a symbol of longevity and purity."

"Oh, thank you!" said Christina. "I will treasure this always." Out of the corner of her eye, she saw Mimi smile. She also saw Mimi give Grant a little bump with her elbow.

"Oh!" said Grant, jumping. "Thank you very much, Mr. and Mrs. Fu." Then in a troubled voice, he added, "It is just the color of his eyes."

"Whose eyes?" asked Mrs. Fu, confused.

The other kids looked at Grant. They knew exactly who he was talking about.

"Uh, Buddha, I think," said Grant, "or is it Confucius?"

The adults laughed, thinking Grant had made a joke, but the kids did not join in.

Soon, more tea was served and a dessert of fruit was brought to the table, along with a single fortune cookie, placed in front of Grant. The waiter, all in black, looked directly into

Grant's eyes. He raised his thick, black eyebrows and gave the frightened boy a little smile as if to say, *"How do you like this turn of events...you cannot escape me anywhere you go."*

"Yeah," said Grant, "jade green is exactly the color of his eyes."

The adults laughed again at the curious little boy, always making jokes and teasing them.

"Grant, I don't see how you have the good luck to always get a fortune cookie," said Mimi merrily. "Open it and read us your fortune."

Glumly, Grant did just that. He opened the note and read: "Let's go to the Great Wall."

"That's a strange fortune," said Papa.

"I think maybe it's not a fortune," Christina said, trying to help.

"Then what is it?" asked Mimi, confused.

"I think it might just be a really, really good idea?" said Christina.

"Oh!" said the Fus, "You have not seen the Great Wall yet?"

"We've been too busy so far," said Mimi. "But we will go soon."

Grant swallowed hard. *He just hoped it was soon enough!*

Leaving Kowloon

Soon it was time to return to Hong Kong and their hotel. Li and Cong stayed in Kowloon to spend the night with their parents at their hotel. "We will bring our children to you in the morning on our way to work," said Mr. Fu.

Reluctantly, the kids said goodbye to one another at the ferry terminal. Once aboard, Grant and Christina waved at Li and Cong until they were finally just two small dots on the dock.

Mimi and Papa had gone up to the upper deck to sit down. Christina and Grant stayed downstairs on the main deck. When their grandparents were out of sight, Christina asked, "Grant, that's not what your fortune cookie message really said, right?"

"Right," said Grant, "but I couldn't read the real message, so I thought maybe I'd give Mimi and Papa a big hint that we should go to the Great Wall. I'm afraid we are going to run out of time before we get to try to find the treasure and solve this mystery, aren't you?"

Christina sighed. "Yeah, I am. I know how carried away Mimi and Papa can get. They might just say, 'Oh, we'll see it next time.'"

"Surely not," said Grant, "not something like the Great Wall!" He looked very dismayed.

"Well, what did the real message say?" asked Christina impatiently.

"I said I couldn't read it," grumbled Grant.

Christina didn't understand. "Grant, you can read!"

Grant pulled the paper from his pocket and shoved it under his sister's face. "Well, I can't read THIS!"

"Oh," said Christina **dejectedly**.

Grant looked around the deck. "Do you think the man followed us this time?"

The man had followed them everywhere so far, Christina thought, but she did not want her little brother to be scared. So she put her arm around him and said, "No, Grant, I think he probably had to stay behind and wash all those dishes."

That thought made Grant giggle, but he didn't look like he believed his sister. He just stared out to sea. They both were sleepy and tired, but at least now they had two jade good-luck charms to keep them company. *Didn't they?*

Good Luck Charms

The next morning, Christina and Grant were pleasantly surprised to hear Papa say, "We are going to the Great Wall!"

Both kids were speechless with excitement. When Papa returned to his bedroom, Christina and Grant both bent over and put their hands over their mouths to suppress their giggles.

"Christina!" whispered Grant, "It worked! That note was a good hint and the good luck charms must have helped, too!"

Christina stood up and laughed out loud. "Maybe so, Grant. At least we're going to get to go to the Great Wall after all!"

Just then Papa returned from the bedroom. He wore a grim face.

"Uh, oh," said Christina, "what's wrong, Papa?" She feared he had changed his mind.

Papa shook his head. "Mimi isn't coming with us. She's sick. She says maybe it's something she ate last night or perhaps she caught a cold, or even the flu, on the airplane. She wants us to go on while she recuperates."

Christina felt like crying. "But it won't be the same without Mimi!"

Grant surprised his sister and grandfather by insisting, "Sure it will. I mean, it'll be OK. She can get well and we can take pictures and show her everything." He hung his head and looked like he might cry.

"Grant!" said Christina.

"No, no, it's ok," said Mimi. She stood at the bedroom door, looking like she felt just awful. She wore the hotel's thick terrycloth bathrobe and hugged a box of tissues to her chest. "There's no sense me giving you guys germs. I'll just rest and read. But if you don't go on, then I'm afraid we will run out of time. It's just one of those things."

"Oh, Mimi," said Christina, "I'm sorry."

"Me...me....me....*AHCHOOOO!*...too," said Mimi. Then she waved and blew a kiss and headed back to bed.

Papa sighed. "Well, the good news is, Li and Cong are downstairs waiting. So let's go." He returned to the bedroom to tuck Mimi in and call room service for orange juice and toast. "Go on down and I'll catch up with you," he called from the bedroom.

Grant and Christina grabbed their backpacks and ran for the elevator.

"I'll bet this will be the shortest trip to the Great Wall ever," said Christina. "Papa will not leave poor Mimi alone for long, especially since she's sick."

When the elevator doors opened, Li and Cong greeted them with a squeal.

"Hello, pen pals," said Li, giving Christina a hug. "What's new?"

"Grant has a new clue," said Christina.

"We know," said Cong. "He read it to us last night at dinner."

"No," said Christina, "he made that up. Grant, show them the real clue and see if they can read it."

Grant pulled the paper from his pocket.

"It's in Chinese," he said, "so Christina and I can't read it."

Cong laughed. "That's not Chinese. Not really. It's just written in calligraphy."

Christina looked over his shoulder. "Oh, I see now! Look, Grant, and you can make out the letters, too!"

Using his forefinger, Grant slowly traced the letters. At first he still couldn't read the word, then suddenly—like a puzzle becoming clear—he began to read the letters of the word aloud.

"B...

... E...

... W...

... A...

... R...

... E...

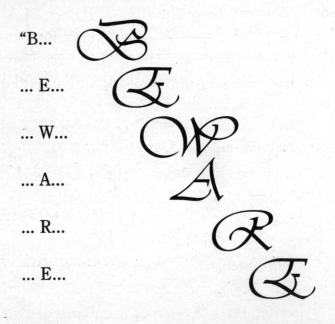

Beware!

"Beware!" Grant said.

"Beware?" repeated Cong. "That can't be good."

"*Bewaaaaare,*" drawled Li in dismay.

"Beware," repeated Christina forlornly.

Grant wondered if they were all deaf. "Beware!" he said. "I said BEWARE!"

Just as he shouted this, the elevator door opened and there stood Papa. He gave Grant a big frown. "If Mimi was here, she'd warn *you* to beware, young man."

"It's a game, Papa," Christina volunteered. "We were just solving a puzzle."

"Is your grandmother not coming with us to the Great Wall?" asked Li.

"No," said Christina. "She's very sick. She's staying here."

"Oh," said Cong, sadly. "I guess she can't write a mystery with us in it if she is sick, can she?"

Christina smiled. "Mimi can write a mystery in rain or sleet or snow or hurricane or earthquake or..."

"No, no, no!" corrected Papa. "Mimi is sick and I shut her computer down and put it away. She is supposed to rest." He looked at Li and Cong. "Your mother is going to check on her until we get back."

Suddenly, all the children were silent.

"Hey, what's wrong?" asked Papa. "I thought everyone was dying to go to the Great Wall."

"Don't say *dying,* please, Papa," said Grant.

But his grandfather just ignored him as he fished in his pocket. "Aha! Our train tickets. Let's go, and cheer up—Mimi wants us to have fun!"

The kids followed Papa out of the hotel. As they started down the street, Christina looked back and saw Mimi's blurry figure in a window. It looked like she was dabbing at her eyes with a tissue.

The kids had to walk double-time down the street to keep up with Papa's long stride. Everyone stared at the man in the cowboy hat and cowboy boots. Papa gave them each a big smile. "I'm breaking trail for you," he called back to the kids, "so keep up little doggies. Chop-chop!"

"Your Papa is silly," said Li, as she walked faster.

"Tell us about it!" said Christina. But she felt safe knowing that Papa would be with them at the Great Wall.

As they walked to the train station, Christina took in all the amazing and exotic sights. A beautiful temple with a fancy roof was painted bright yellow. The sweet smell of incense wafted through the air. An outdoor market was piled high with carpets, stacks of many-tentacled squid, strange fruits, and even songbirds in cages—all for sale to the many shoppers who bargained for a good price—*jiangjia*, Li called it.

Soon they began to ride escalator after escalator.

"Is this the world's longest escalator?" asked Grant in amazement.

"As a matter of fact, it is," said Cong. "It is called The Escalator and it's the longest covered outdoor one in the world!"

Finally, they exited The Escalator and soon were at the train station, barely in time to climb aboard before the train began to chug out of the station.

Papa settled back with his newspaper and tea, giving the kids some *yuan* for lunch when they were ready. For hours and hours they watched the incredible and endless landscape of China pass by their windows.

After they got out of the city, they saw forests of waving bamboo, ancient walled villages, wide yellow rivers, deep gorges, bearded mountain goats, hillside terraces where rice was growing, water buffalo, forests of oddly-shaped stone called *karst*, and people doing exercise called *tai ji quan* in the open air.

Christina thought it was all so magically different from the things she was familiar with back home, which is why, she guessed, travel was so mysterious and so much fun to her. She wished they could go to Tibet, which she knew was called the "Roof of the World" and see

Mt. Everest, the world's tallest mountain, or ride the Trans-Siberian Express all the way to Moscow, Russia. Mimi told Christina she had the "travel bug," just like she did, and Christina guessed that it was true.

She turned to ask the other kids if they were ready for a snack. But when she looked, Papa was sprawled back with his cowboy hat over his face, which only barely muffled his snoring. Li, Cong, and Grant were tumbled over like puppies, sound asleep, using one another as pillows.

Soon, Christina dozed and dreamed. So, she did not see the man pass by, stop, and smile a smug smile as if he was having a very lucky day.

Missing!

It was very late afternoon. Or was it even the next morning? Christina was not sure. She was sore from sleeping in such an awkward position. As she pushed up and stretched, she noticed the most awful thing— Grant was not there.

Quickly, she shook Li and Cong. "Wake up!" she whispered, not wanting to disturb Papa. "Grant's gone! Have you seen him?"

Cong yawned. "How can we see him if he is gone?"

Li stretched. "Maybe he went to the bathroom?"

Christina felt the butterflies in her stomach settle down a little. Maybe he did, she thought, but she did not feel so certain. Without another word, she clambered over Li and Cong and made her way down the aisle. Most people were sleeping, or starting to wake up.

She walked as quickly as the weaving, bobbing train allowed and looked at each seat she passed. After walking through six cars, she was really worried and about to head back to get Papa, when she spied Grant's sneakers peeking out into the aisle from a seat. He was not moving.

Frightened, she dashed to the seat and found her brother curled up, sound asleep. He seemed to be all right except for one very strange thing—all the pockets of his pants and jacket had been turned inside out!

"Grant! Grant!" Christina said. Nearby sleepy passengers stretched and grumbled. "Wake up! Are you ok?"

Grant struggled to sit up. "I'm fine, just sleepy. What's all the fuss about? Are we there yet?" He rubbed his eyes.

Christina glanced out the window. "I don't know," she said, "but look!" She point to Grant's clothing.

Grant looked down and grinned.

"What's so funny?" Christina demanded. "Why did you wander off?"

Now Grant was fully alert. "I didn't," he said. "I must have sleepwalked...or someone moved me!"

The brother and sister stared at one another in shock.

"You don't think..." Christina began.

"It has to be," Grant finished.

Christina gasped. "Then he got your map! Look at your pockets!"

Grant grinned. "No he didn't. Look in *your* pocket."

Confused, Christina reached into her jacket pocket. Then she smiled. "What made you do that?" she asked.

Grant shook his head. "I just had this funny feeling in my dream," he said. "And I woke up and thought about putting the map in your pocket instead...just in case, you know."

"Good thing!" said Christina. "But, come on...fix your pockets and let's get back before Papa wakes up."

As the kids hopped up from the seat and hurried back through the cars, the man came out of the bathroom and saw them. Even though they were not looking his way, he shook his fist at them.

The Great Wall

"Great Wall...Great Wall!" cried the train porter. The train lurched to a stop and people began to gather their things.

"Hurry up," said Papa, barely awake. "We are only here an hour and then we take the train on into Beijing."

"An hour?" said Christina.

"Just an hour?" asked Cong, with a groan.

"Only an hour, sir?" Li asked.

"One measly hour," Grant said with a groan.

But Papa just ignored them as he yawned and stretched. Then he led them down the aisle and off of the train.

The sun was already thinking about going down. But it was still quite bright out, with shadows deepening in the mountain valleys. As soon as the kids spied the Great Wall they cheered!

"It really, really is great!" said Grant. He pointed up the mountain. "It looks like it goes on forever!"

They could see that some of the wall had been restored while other parts were crumbled ruins. They could also see that the treasure map really was about the Great Wall. The only problem was just that: the wall was GREAT, and their time was short.

Papa headed for a coffee vendor, which gave the kids a chance to look closely at the map. Christina thought about what Mimi had taught her about solving mysteries. *Look past the red herrings,* she had said. *Think logically. Focus on the possible. Put your mind in the mind of the criminal.*

"What do you think?" asked Grant. He knew his sister was good at solving puzzles.

"Let's just be quiet a minute and *look*," Christina suggested. "And see what we can see."

Slowly, like a hidden picture puzzle, the kids began to draw some interesting conclusions about the map.

For one thing, the X's corresponded to specific features of the restored part of the Great Wall.

"See," said Christina. "There are no X's anywhere on the carriageway, as the signs say the part of the wall you walk on is called. And that makes sense—you probably wouldn't hide treasure where anyone could just stumble upon it."

"But there's an X on this watchtower," said Cong. "Maybe the treasure is hidden in one of them? You know," he added, "these were used like forts and storerooms. And of course, soldiers kept watch from those high positions."

Nervously, the kids looked up at the tall tower. Could anyone be watching them from up there, they wondered. There were few tourists this late in the afternoon. But the tower was walled, and anyone could easily hide behind the **ramparts**.

"There's an X here," said Li. She pointed
to a nearby signal beacon where dried wolf dung
was once burned to warn of impending attacks.
"So maybe there is some treasure there?"

Grant was quiet. He kept looking at the
last X on the map. He walked over to look at a
diagram of how the wall was constructed. He
could see that it was filled with large stones,
brick, earth, rubble, and, the sign said, a mixture
of lime and rice that worked like concrete to seal
the mixture all together.

Grant thought it was rather odd that rice
and lime juice would become as hard as

concrete.   But as he continued reading, he learned that "lime" is limestone that had been crushed into a powder. It is still an ingredient in cement.

He looked back at the X. It was just drawn on the side of the wall, almost as if it was in no special place. But somehow, he felt that might be where the treasure was. He was afraid to go up in the watchtower. The mean man could be up there. And he sure didn't want to dig around in any dried animal poop to look for treasure, if he could help it!

X Marks the Spot!

Grant returned to where the other kids were standing. "I think we should try to wander over there," he said, pointing to the X on the wall on the map.

"Time is running out," Christina agreed. "We may only have enough time to try one of the X's. And if we choose the wrong one...well, I guess that will be the end of that."

The kids stared at the Great Wall so hard they did not hear Papa come up behind them. "Hey!" he said, startling them. "I have a great Great Wall story I've been meaning to tell you."

"Uh, could you tell us later?" Grant asked, standing on one foot and then the other.

"Oh, you'll want to hear this one," said Papa. "It's about a famous American fighter pilot named Bob Scott. After he returned from World War II, he got the idea that he wanted to walk the Great Wall of China."

"You mean part of it, right?" asked Cong.

"Nope!" said Papa, waving his arms back and forth. "He wanted to walk the whole thing! And he did, too! It took him an entire year. And before he left home, he baked himself 1,000 special, extra-healthy chocolate chip cookies— and that's what he ate while he walked!"

"Great story," said Li.

"Really good story," said Christina. "Can we walk on the Great Wall now?"

"Of course!" said Papa. "You mean you haven't been up there yet? There isn't much time before the train leaves, better hurry. Oops!" he said, suddenly, looking all around. "I forgot the backpacks in the gift shop where I was buying Mimi a souvenir. I'll be right back or meet you over there." He pointed toward the path to the train station.

"OK," said Christina. "Take your time, Papa," she encouraged her grandfather.

As soon as he was out of earshot, the kids devised a plan. "Look," said Grant. "I'm going to wander over to the wall. Christina, you stand back here with the map and guide me left or right to where you think the X seems to be located on the map. Cong, you watch the watchtower. And Li, will you please keep an eye out for Papa?"

The kids nodded eagerly. They knew it was a long shot that Grant would find any treasure, but it was fun to try and to pretend that they might have good fortune.

Grant took a big gulp of air, as if he were going underwater. Then, bravely, he marched toward the side of the wall. Every now and then, he would look back at Christina. She would motion to him with her hand whether to move left or right. The only problem was, she kept changing her mind.

Finally, exasperated, Grant ran all the way back. Out of breath, he asked, "What gives? You keep moving me back and forth."

"Well, it's hard, Grant," grumbled Christina. "It's not like there's some big, giant X up there on the wall, you know."

Then, suddenly, Christina got a peculiar look on her face. *Ignore all the red herrings,* she

reminded herself. *See what others don't see.*
These were the things Mimi had told her about
solving mysteries. She squealed. "There *is* an X,
there *is* an X!" she said.

The other kids stared at the wall.
"Where?" said Li. "I do not see any X."

"I do not think you should tease us,
Christina," said Cong. "There is not time for that."

But Grant just looked at his sister. He
knew that if she said she saw an X on the wall that
she meant it. But no matter how hard he stared
and squinted, he could see nothing but blank wall.

"Look!" Christina said, pointing to the
map then to the wall. "If you draw an imaginary
line with your eye from the X on the watchtower
to the X on the signal beacon...like this..." She
moved her finger across the map. "Then you
draw an imaginary line from the watchtower to
the wall and from the signal beacon to the wall,
the lines intersect...and..."

"And form a triangle!" said Grant. "And right there...(he pointed to a spot on the map) is exactly where the X—and the treasure!—should be!"

"*Should be*," said Li, "but can it really be true?"

"Uh, I think it might be," said Cong in a nervous voice. "Look!"

As the kids followed where Cong pointed, up at the watchtower, they saw the mean man stick his head out between the ramparts. He shook his finger at them.

"Oh, brother," said Grant. "He's figured out that we've figured out where the treasure is."

"Only he has one big advantage," said Christina.

"What's that?" asked Li.

"He knows *what* the treasure is!" said Christina. "We don't actually have a clue what we are looking for!"

A Race to the Treasure!

The man begin to run down the carriageway to get down off the wall. As he ran, they could see his black jacket fling open and reveal the yellow lining.

"Hurry, Grant!" shouted Cong. "We will hold him off!"

Grant began to run toward the wall. He still had to look back as Christina directed him, but this time she pointed her finger to a very precise point on the wall.

When Grant ran, the man began to run faster. Grant heard the other kids squeal behind him. People were beginning to stare at them.

"Why did you tell Grant we would hold the man off?" Christina asked Cong. "We can't do that, you know!"

"We can try!" said Li and Cong together and they began to run. They surprised Christina by running directly toward the man.

Christina turned and looked at her brother. He was at the wall. He looked so tiny and helpless beside the enormous wall. She could tell that he was looking and looking. He ran his hand over the stones of the wall. Then suddenly, he ducked. The man was throwing rocks at him!

Li and Cong tried to stop the man by running up to him and asking him rapid-fire questions in Chinese, while making kung fu moves. But the man just brushed them aside and ran right past them. As he ran, he stooped to pick up more stones to throw at Grant.

"Hey, cut that out!" yelled Christina. "That's my brother."

The man ran right past, ignoring her. Then, suddenly, he skidded on some rubble and fell flat on his back. The kids could tell that this knocked the breath out of him.

"Hurry, Grant! Hurry!" they cried.

But Grant was paying no attention to anyone. The last rock that the man had thrown had hit one stone in the wall and loosened it. With his small fingers, Grant was able to pry the stone away. He could see a wad of plastic wrapper inside and began to pull and tug to get the package out from in between the rocks.

The man finally got up and began to run even faster toward Grant. Grant pulled and tugged. At last, the package popped out of its hiding place. Grant held it tight and began to run back toward the other kids. He tried to stay as far from the man as possible, but the man made a quick turn and grabbed the package out of his hand.

"Your good luck is up!" the man said in a breathless mean voice. "Now, scram, kid, before I call the authorities."

Suddenly, Grant and the man both froze, for behind them a booming voice said, "YOU DON'T STEAL FROM KIDS, BUDDY!!"

"Papa!" Christina screamed. "Thank goodness you're here!"

The man was so surprised to see a cowboy at the Great Wall that just for a moment, he was speechless and did not move. When he seemed to realize that this cowboy was just someone with the children, he snarled at them all and began to run away out of their reach.

But then they all heard another booming voice, "STOP! We know who you are! You are under arrest!"

Everyone froze! The kids thought that the man in the uniform meant them, perhaps. After all, they had now defaced the Great Wall of China. Even Papa thought he might be in trouble. After all, he had yelled at a Chinese citizen. But the uniformed man, who wore a gun on his hip, walked directly up to the man in the black jacket.

"You, jade thief," the officer said. "You are under arrest!" He yanked the plastic-wrapped package from the man's hands and gave it to Papa to hold while he handcuffed the man.

But the kids knew who was really in trouble. "*Graaaaant!*" Papa said. "*Christinaaaaa!*"

The Jade Thief

Other officers soon rushed up and took the thief away. Then the officers turned to Papa.

"Sir?" one said, with a suspicious tone in his voice. "We would like to know exactly, please, how you knew about this package."

Everyone stared at Papa. Finally Papa said, "You mean this isn't a peanut butter and jelly sandwich in this wrapper you handed to me?" He gave a nervous laugh.

Grant came forward and tugged on his grandfather's sleeve. "Uh, Papa, I think we can explain. There might be some kind of treasure in there."

The stern-looking officers began to laugh. "Might be?" said one. "Let's look and see, please." He took the package and laid it on a large flat stone on the ground. He began to gently unwrap the package. With each pull and tug of the wrapper, the kids drew closer and closer.

Finally the wrapper fell away to reveal a large handful of beautiful green pieces of pure jade. Just then sunlight spewed through one of the Great Wall's ramparts and shined on the jade stones, causing them to glint like tiger eyes.

"I told you," Grant said quietly, "just the color of the bad guy's eyes."

"The bad guy, as you call him," said one of the officers, "is the infamous jade thief that has been in all the newspapers. Have you tourists not read about this?"

Papa shook his head. "We just briefly heard about it from these children's (he indicated Li and Cong) parents the other night. They export fine jade pieces."

The officers looked suspicious once again. "And do they have anything to do with this theft?"

"Oh, no!" said Li. "They were just worried about all the museum pieces being stolen, perhaps never to be found again."

Now the officers looked very confused. One officer waved his hands around in the air. "And so, how, how exactly did you know that this man and this treasure was here? Help me, please, to understand."

Papa looked at Grant and Christina. "You heard the officer," he said sternly. "Help him—help *me*—please, to understand. Now."

The four children looked at one another and they just couldn't help it. They began to laugh! And once they started laughing, they just could not stop.

Papa and the officers looked very befuddled and aggravated. "What is so funny?" Papa finally demanded.

"I'm sorry," Christina sputtered. "But we just know—" she had to stop and giggle again— "We just know that you won't believe that Grant found a treasure map on the airplane and—"

"A TREASURE MAP?!" boomed Papa. "Now *that's* a likely story. You kids have more imagination than Mimi if you expect me to believe—"

Before his grandfather could finish his tirade, Grant quickly pulled the map from his pocket and handed it to Papa. Papa stared at it, speechless. He handed it to the chief officer, who stared at it, speechless. They all stared at the map then they all stared at the wall then they all stared at the children—who started giggling all over again.

How You Gonna Keep 'Em Down on the Farm, After They've Seen the Great Wall?

The next morning, four tired, dirty, hungry kids stood in Mimi's bedroom in the hotel. She looked much better and was all dressed in a pretty red suit and had her hair fixed, but she still hugged the filthy children until they thought she would squash them flat.

After all the events at the Great Wall, they had been allowed to get on the train just as it was about to leave the station. They had traveled all night, arrived back in Hong Kong, and been escorted directly to Mimi's room by Papa, who looked like a pretty tired, dirty cowboy himself.

Mimi beamed. "It's in all the newspapers this morning!" she said. "You kids captured the Jade Thief! The phone has been ringing off the hook with reporters calling here. I just don't understand."

Grant showed Mimi the treasure map and she looked puzzled. Then her eyes gleamed. "Grant!" she said, "you won't believe this..."

Before she could finish, Cong interrupted her. "I see your computer is open on your desk," he said. "Did you decide to write a mystery?"

Once more Mimi beamed. "I did!" she said. "I was sleeping and I had the strangest dream. I dreamed that there was a treasure map and some missing jade, and..."

Now Christina interrupted. "Oh, Mimi, you did not. You're making that up—aren't you?"

Mimi shook her blond curls. "I promise I'm not," she said. "I just got this great idea for a story...how could I have known that it would come true?"

Papa shook his head and looked at his grandkids. "Truth is stranger than fiction," he said.

"Are we in the book?" Li asked eagerly.

Mimi laughed. "Why, you and Cong are our Number One Chinese pen pals—of course you are!"

All the kids laughed, squealed, and jumped up and down.

"I'm taking these treasure-hunting varmints downstairs to get some breakfast," said Papa. He handed Mimi a package. "Bought you a souvenir at the Great Wall."

"Oh, thank you, dear," said Mimi. She tore off the wrapper and discovered a beautiful jade tiger. She gave Papa a funny look. "This isn't...." she began.

"No," Papa promised. "We did not get to keep the treasure, we just got to find it, and how, well, I'll never know." He gave Grant a funny look.

Suddenly, the door to their suite burst open. "Our heroes!" said the head of the hotel. He was followed by waiters and waitresses, onlookers, and Li's and Cong's parents. The hotel staff and some of the onlookers kowtowed to the four kids by kneeling and lowering their heads to the floor.

The hotel manager said, "We have brought gifts to the treasure-hunting children."

He presented a large silver tray filled with sweets and fruit. From his pocket he pulled a special item and handed it to Grant. It was a fortune cookie.

Grant slapped his forehead. "Aw, man," he said. "I don't think I can take any more good luck just yet, *please!?*"

About the Author

Carole Marsh is an author and publisher who has written many works of fiction and non-fiction for young readers. She travels throughout the United States and around the world to research her books. In 1979 Carole Marsh was named Communicator of the Year for her corporate communications work with major national and international corporations.

Marsh is the founder and CEO of Gallopade International, established in 1979. Today, Gallopade International is widely recognized as a leading source of educational materials for every state and many countries. Marsh and Gallopade were recipients of the 2004 Teachers' Choice Award. Marsh has written more than 50 Carole Marsh Mysteries™. Years ago, her children, Michele and Michael, were the original characters in her mystery books. Today, they continue the Carole Marsh Books tradition by working at Gallopade. By adding grandchildren Grant and Christina as new mystery characters, she has continued the tradition for a third generation.

Ms. Marsh welcomes correspondence from her readers. You can e-mail her at fanclub@gallopade.com, visit the carolemarshmysteries.com website, or write to her in care of Gallopade International, P.O. Box 2779, Peachtree City, Georgia, 30269 USA.

Built-In Book Club

Talk About It!

1. Have you ever eaten a fortune cookie? Do you remember what was written on the piece of paper inside?

2. Cong mentioned that the man following him had a scar over his eyebrow. What are some other things about a person that you might notice in order to recognize him or her again?

3. Have you ever seen or used an abacus? If so, did you think it was a smart way to solve math problems?

4. When you read that Grant was not going to return the map as he was instructed in the fortune cookie note, did you think that was a good idea or a bad idea? Why?

5. Even though Grant and Christina and Li and Cong were from different countries, they became fast friends. What things do kids all over the world have in common?

6. Do you have the "travel bug" like Christina and Mimi? If so, where would you like to visit?

7. What does it mean to have "butterflies in your stomach?" Why did Christina feel them when Grant was missing?

8. Why were all the pockets in Grant's clothing turned inside out when Christina found him sleeping on the train?

9. The Great Wall of China is the world's longest man-made structure—almost 4,000 miles long! How would you prefer to see it—fly over it in an airplane or walk along it? Why?

10. If you wrote your own "real kids/real places" international mystery, what country would you choose for the setting? Why?

Built-In Book Club

Bring it to Life!

1. Ask a volunteer to draw a map of China on a large piece of poster board. Do you remember when Papa said that China covers 50 degrees of latitude? On a globe or map of the world, find China and identify its latitudes. Draw them on your China map. Then, mark the capital city of Beijing with a red star. Finally, draw the Great Wall on your map.

2. Draw a fireworks display with crayons or markers! Make it colorful and creative— remember, the Chinese love fireworks!

3. Enjoy a Chinese feast! Ask parents to volunteer to bring in Chinese food. You can ask for egg rolls, lo mein, fried rice, a stir-fry dish

with meat and vegetables, dim sum—whatever you like! Make sure you get some green tea to drink, and fortune cookies for dessert.

4. Make your own "fortune cookies." First, cut some strips of paper and write fortunes on them. Next, cut pieces of paper into squares that are four inches wide by four inches long. Fold the squares into triangles. Put the fortunes inside them. You can tape or glue the sides of your fortune cookie. Pass them around the room and see who gets each fortune!

5. Create some good luck charms of your own. Bring in colored bars of soap. Carve animals out of the soap to create your own special charms!

6. Build the Great Wall of China! Find a large piece of cardboard. Use modeling clay, popsicle sticks, blocks, dominoes, Legos®, or whatever else you can think of to build a model of the Great Wall. Don't forget to add the watchtowers, and maybe a few tourists walking around!

Glossary

 accompany: to go with a companion

bustling: full of energetic and noisy activity

chinnoserie: Chinese-style decoration or object popular in the 17th and 18th centuries in Europe

chop: seal or stamp used in east Asia to prove identity

dejectedly: in a depressed or sad manner

dynasty: a ruling family that remains in power for generations

funicular railway: a railway up the side of a mountain pulled by a moving cable

incense: substance that produces a fragrant odor when burned

marvel: to be amazed at

Ming dynasty: the imperial dynasty of China from 1368 to 1644

rampart: a stone or earth wall protecting a city or town

red herring: something used to draw attention away from the real issue

terracotta: brown-orange clay used to make many items including figurines, pottery, and roof tiles

Would you ~~MYSTERIES~~ like to be
a character in a Carole Marsh Mystery?

If you would like to star in a Carole Marsh Mystery, fill out the form below and write a 25-word paragraph about why you think you would make a good character! Once you're done, ask your mom or dad to send this page to:

Carole Marsh Mysteries Fan Club
Gallopade International
P.O. Box 2779
Peachtree City, GA 30269

My name is:

I am a:_____boy _____ girl   Age:_____ _____

I live at: _____

City:_____ State:_____ Zip code:_____

My e-mail address: _____

My phone number is: _____

_____

_____

_____

_____

_____

_____

_____

_____

_____

Visit the <u>carolemarshmysteries.com</u> website to:

- Join the Carole Marsh Mysteries™ Fan Club!

- Write a letter to Christina, Grant, Mimi, or Papa!

- Cast your vote for where the next mystery should take place!

- Find fascinating facts about the countries where the mysteries take place!

- Track your reading on an international map!

- Take the Fact or Fiction online quiz!

- Play the Around-the-World Scavenger Hunt computer game!

- Find out where the *Mystery Girl* is flying next!